THI BLOOMSBURY BOOK

BELONGS TO

....

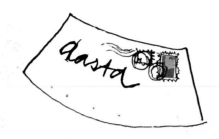

To my own Bjorn.

First published in Great Britain in 1999 by Bloomsbury Publishing Plc
38 Soho Square, London, W1D 3HB
This paperback edition first published 2001

A CIP catalogue record of this book is available from the British Library
ISBN 0 7475 5004 2 (Paperback)
ISBN 0 7475 4127 2 (Hardback)

Printed in Hong Kong by South China Printing Co.

1 3 5 7 9 10 8 6 4 2

Princess Aasta

Stina Langlo Ørdal

BLOOMSBURY
CHILDREN'S
BOOKS

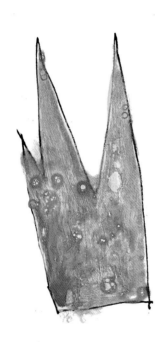

Once upon a time
there was a little princess
called **Aasta,**
who wanted a bear
to love.

She decided to send a letter to a newspaper – "Little princess seeking big, cuddly bear friend".

Shortly afterwards, she received letters from **bears** all over the world.

Black, brown and white **bears,** and even **grizzly bears.**

Princess Aasta was **very excited** and went through

all the letters,

(there were many of them).

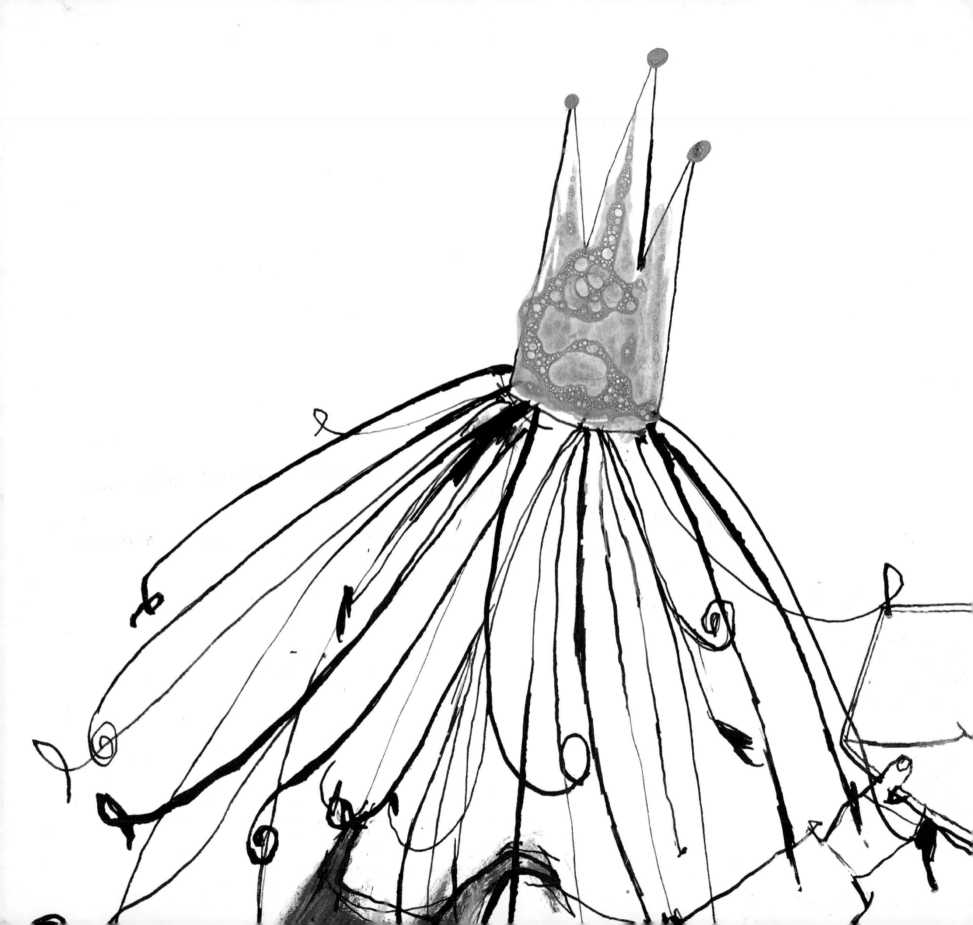

She chose one, Kvitebjørn, who had the friendliest eyes she had ever seen, and sent a letter back to him asking if they could meet some time.

They met in Princess Aasta's apple garden, and chased each other in between the trees.

Kvitebjørn picked apples for Princess Aasta from the top branches.

Princess Aasta and Kvitebjørn wanted to be together always.

The **King**

was worried about having

a **big,** dangerous

Ursus maritimus running about in his

garden.

But when he saw how much

fun the two of them had together,

he left them alone.

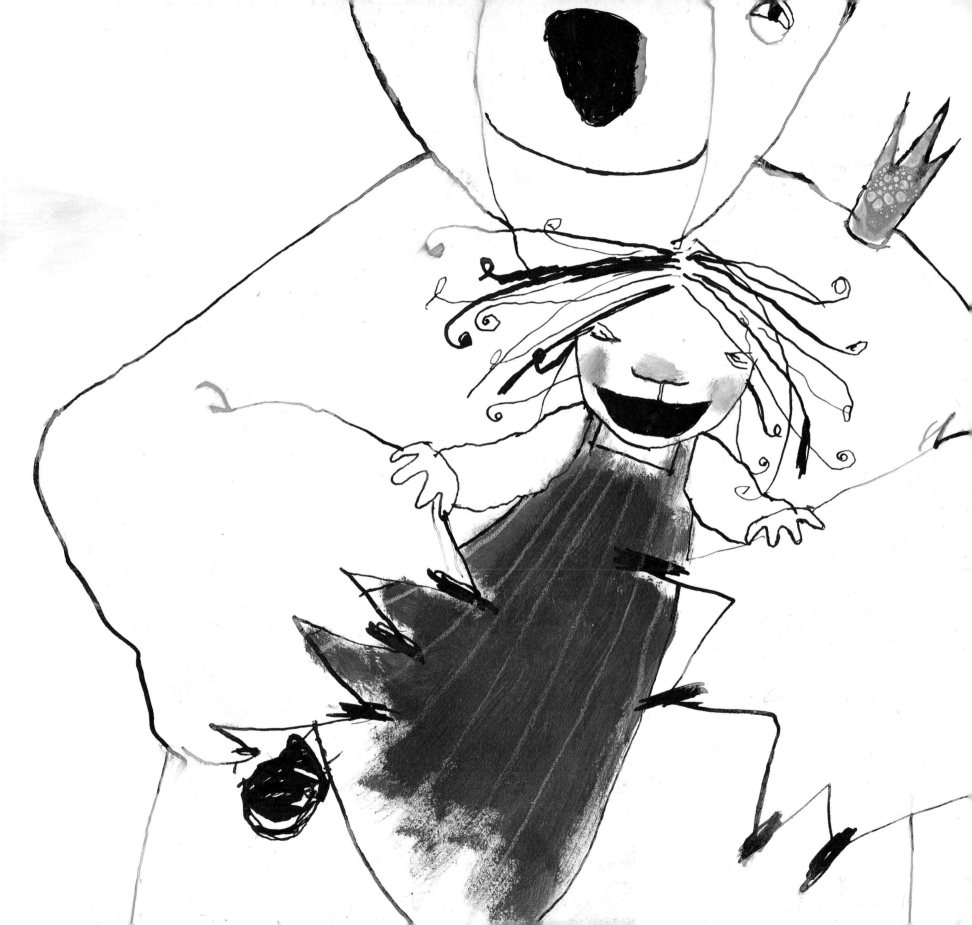

And when Kvitebjørn wanted to take Princess Aasta on a day trip to the North Pole, where he was from, the King couldn't say no.

The King made them a packed lunch, and bade them a safe journey.

Princess Aasta climbed on to Kvitebjørn's back, and off they went, as far north as anyone can get. It was so beautiful up there, everything was covered in ice and snow. And Princess Aasta would never be cold, because Kvitebjørn's fur kept her warm.

Kvitebjørn introduced her to all his polar bear friends.

Afterwards, they went ice-skating and made an enormous snowman together.

And when **northern lights** appeared in the sky, it was time to go back to the King's castle.

The King was waiting for **them** at the door.

He was still a bit scared of Princess Aasta's **huge** polar **bear** friend, **but when** Kvitebjørn bent down and gave him a **huge, warm and cuddly hug,** he felt a bit better and asked if Kvitebjørn would join them for supper.

Acclaim for *Princess Aasta*

'A powerful book about loneliness and love' *The Herald*

'Splendidly scribbly pictures ... and a huggable bear' *Sunday Times*

'This is a bold adventurous book' *Books for Keeps*

Enjoy more great picture books from Bloomsbury ...

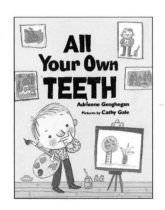

All Your Own Teeth
Adrienne Geoghegan &
Cathy Gale

Five Little Fiends
Sarah Dyer

Tom Finger
Gillian McClure

**Get Busy This
Christmas**
Stephen Waterhouse